Rooster's
Alarm

First published in 2008 by
Franklin Watts
338 Euston Road
London
NW1 3BH

Franklin Watts Australia
Level 17 / 207 Kent Street
Sydney
NSW 2000

A CIP catalogue record for this book is available
from the British Library.

ISBN 978 0 7496 7885 2 (hbk)
ISBN 978 0 7496 7891 3 (pbk)

Series Editor: Jackie Hamley
Series Advisor: Dr Hilary Minns
Series Designer: Peter Scoulding

Printed in China

Franklin Watts is a division of
Hachette Children's Books,
an Hachette Livre UK company.

Rooster's Alarm

by Ian Smith and Sean Julian

Illustrated by Ian Smith

FRANKLIN WATTS
LONDON • SYDNEY

Sean Julian

"I don't like alarm clocks because they wake me up when I still want to be asleep."

JS

Ian Smith

"I set my alarm clock good and early so I can get up and have a nice cup of tea."

"Cock-a-doodle-doo!"
cried the sheep,

Cock-a-doodle-doo!

waking up the animals
who were still asleep.

Cat woke up and opened his eyes.

He began to baa
to his great surprise.

The mouse miaowed,

Miaow!

and the dog said, "Squeak!"

11

Turkey barked,
"Woof!" when he
opened his beak.

Goat yelled, "Moo!"

Moo!

14

So the cow said, "Nay!"

16

But that's what horse was going to say.

So horse said, "Oink!"

Oink!

And pig began to cluck.

Quack! Quack!

20

That made hen
quack, just like duck.

The noises were wrong
all around the farm,

because rooster forgot
to set his alarm!

Zzzz!

Notes for adults

TADPOLES are structured to provide support for newly independent readers. The stories may also be used by adults for sharing with young children.

Starting to read alone can be daunting. **TADPOLES** help by providing visual support and repeating words and phrases. These books will both develop confidence and encourage reading and rereading for pleasure.

If you are reading this book with a child, here are a few suggestions:

1. Make reading fun! Choose a time to read when you and the child are relaxed and have time to share the story.
2. Talk about the story before you start reading. Look at the cover and the blurb. What might the story be about? Why might the child like it?
3. Encourage the child to reread the story, and to retell the story in their own words, using the illustrations to remind them what has happened.
4. Discuss the story and see if the child can relate it to their own experience, or perhaps compare it to another story they know.
5. Give praise! Remember that small mistakes need not always be corrected.

If you enjoyed this book, why not try another TADPOLES story?

Sammy's Secret
978 0 7496 6890 7

Stroppy Poppy
978 0 7496 6893 8

I'm Taller Than You!
978 0 7496 6894 5

Leo's New Pet
978 0 7496 6891 4

Mop Top
978 0 7946 6895 2

Charlie and the Castle
978 0 7496 6896 9

Over the Moon!
978 0 7496 6897 6

Five Teddy Bears
978 0 7496 7292 8

My Sister is a Witch!
978 0 7496 6898 3

Little Troll
978 0 7496 7293 5

The Sad Princess
978 0 7496 7294 2

Runny Honey
978 0 7496 7295 9

Dog Knows Best
978 0 7496 7297 3

Sam's Sunflower
978 0 7496 7298 0

My Big New Bed
978 0 7496 7156 3 (hbk)
978 0 7496 7299 7 (pbk)

My Auntie Susan
978 0 7496 7157 0 (hbk)
978 0 7496 7300 0 (pbk)

Bad Luck, Lucy!
978 0 7496 7158 7 (hbk)
978 0 7496 7302 4 (pbk)

At the End of the Garden
978 0 7496 7159 4 (hbk)
978 0 7496 7303 1 (pbk)

Bertie and the Big Balloon
978 0 7496 7161 7 (hbk)
978 0 7496 7305 5 (pbk)

Pirate Pete
978 0 7496 7160 0 (hbk)
978 0 7496 7304 8 (pbk)